THIS WALKER BOOK BELONGS TO:

_____

_____

_____

_____

For Paul
(who took me back to school)
and to all the children and teachers,
past and present, who have made
my times at Langley School so special,
with warmest love

And also to Plymbridge Woods nearby

First published 1993 by Walker Books Ltd
87 Vauxhall Walk, London SE11 5HJ

This edition published 2003

2 4 6 8 10 9 7 5 3 1

© 1993, 2003 Simon James

The right of Simon James to be identified
as author/illustrator of this work has been
asserted by him in accordance with the
Copyright, Designs and Patents Act 1988

This book has been typeset in Bembo

Printed in China

British Library Cataloguing in Publication Data:
a catalogue record for this book is available
from the British Library

ISBN 0-7445-9804-4

The Wild Woods

Simon James

WALKER BOOKS
AND SUBSIDIARIES
LONDON • BOSTON • SYDNEY

Jess and her grandad saw
a squirrel one day, down by
the Wild Woods.
"I'd like to take him home,"
Jess said.

"You can't keep a squirrel,"
 cried Grandad.
"They're too wild."

"Don't worry Grandad," said Jess,
"I'll look after him."
"But Jess," called Grandad,
"you can't keep a squirrel.
    What are you going to feed him?"

"He likes our sandwiches,"
Jess said.

"But Jess, come back!" shouted Grandad.
"You can't keep a squirrel.
  Where's he going to sleep?"

"I'll make him a bed in
my room," Jess said.

"Hurry up, Grandad!" said Jess.
"Come and see. I think I've
found a waterfall."

"Jess, you can't really keep a
    squirrel," whispered Grandad.
"I know," said Jess.
"He belongs to the wild."

"I love being in the wild,"
Jess said. "Can we come
back tomorrow?"
"Well… OK," sighed Grandad.
"If we really have to."
"Good," Jess said, "because …

one of those
ducks might need
looking after."